THE
SNOWY
DAY

EZRA JACK KEATS

THE SNOWY DAY

New York · The Viking Press

VIKING
Published by Penguin Group
Penguin Young Readers Group, 345 Hudson Street, New York, New York 10014, U.S.A.
Penguin Group (Canada), 90 Eglinton Avenue East, Suite 700, Toronto, Ontario, Canada M4P 2Y3
(a division of Pearson Penguin Canada Inc.)
Penguin Books Ltd, 80 Strand, London WC2R 0RL, England
Penguin Ireland, 25 St Stephen's Green, Dublin 2, Ireland (a division of Penguin Books Ltd)
Penguin Group (Australia), 250 Camberwell Road, Camberwell, Victoria 3124, Australia
(a division of Pearson Australia Group Pty Ltd)
Penguin Books India Pvt Ltd, 11 Community Centre, Panchsheel Park, New Delhi – 110 017, India
Penguin Group (NZ), 67 Apollo Drive, Rosedale, Auckland 0632, New Zealand
(a division of Pearson New Zealand Ltd)
Penguin Books (South Africa) (Pty) Ltd, 24 Sturdee Avenue, Rosebank, Johannesburg 2196, South Africa

The Snowy Day first published in 1962 by The Viking Press
This edition published in 2011 by Viking, a division of Penguin Young Readers Group

1 3 5 7 9 10 8 6 4 2

The Snowy Day copyright © Ezra Jack Keats, 1962
Additional material copyright © Penguin Group (USA) Inc., 2011
All rights reserved

Page 38, photo of Keats and *Life* magazine images; page 39, manuscript; page 40, letters and photo;
page 41, letter and drawings; page 42, Caldecott medal; page 43, photo and invitation; page 44, photos:
courtesy of the de Grummond Children's Literature Collection, McCain Library and Archives,
University of Southern Mississippi Libraries. Page 39, sketch by Ezra Jack Keats, © Ezra Jack Keats Foundation, 2002.
Page 42, telegram from the files of Viking Children's Books.

LIBRARY OF CONGRESS CATALOGING-IN-PUBLICATION DATA
Keats, Ezra Jack.
The snowy day / by Ezra Jack Keats. — 50th anniversary special ed.
p. cm.
Summary: The adventures of a little boy in the city on a very snowy day.
ISBN 978-0-670-01270-1 (hardcover)
[1. Snow—Fiction. 2. African Americans—Fiction.] I. Title.
PZ7.K2253Sn 2011
[E]—dc22
2010049516

Manufactured in China

To Tick, John, and Rosalie

One winter morning Peter woke up
and looked out the window. Snow
had fallen during the night. It cov-
ered everything as far as he could see.

After breakfast he put on his snowsuit and ran outside. The snow was piled up very high along the street to make a path for walking.

Crunch, crunch, crunch, his feet sank into the snow.
He walked with his toes pointing out, like this:

He walked with his toes
pointing in, like that:

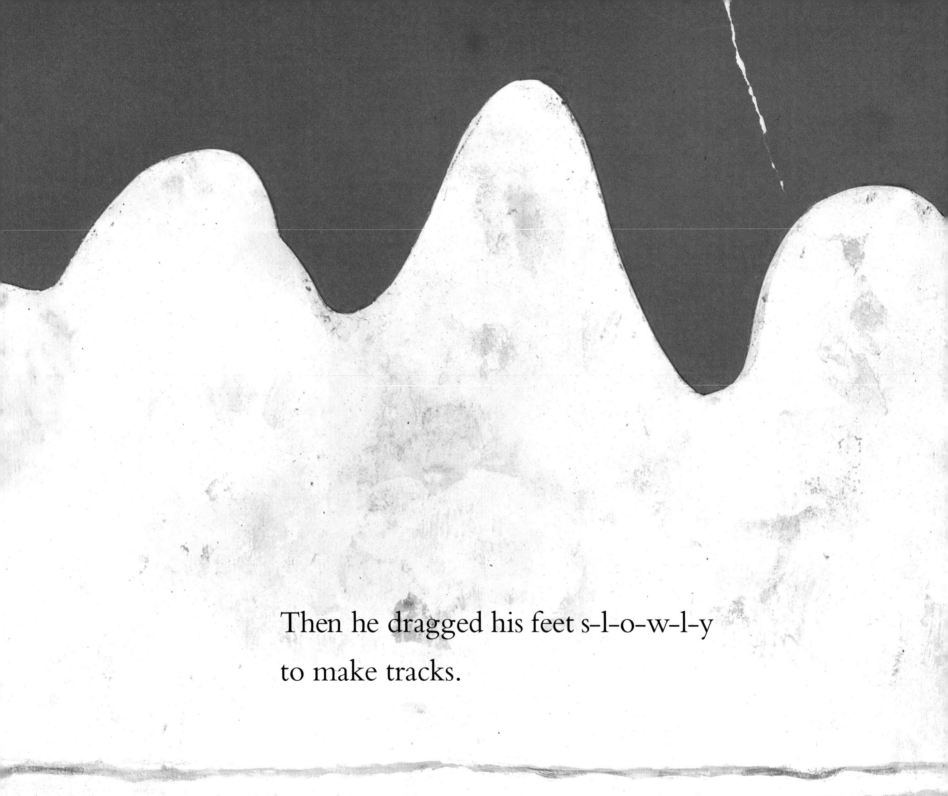

Then he dragged his feet s–l–o–w–l–y
to make tracks.

And he found something sticking out
of the snow that made a new track.

It was a stick

— a stick that was just right for smacking a snow-covered tree.

Down fell the snow —
plop!
— on top of Peter's head.

He thought it would be fun to join the big boys in their snowball fight, but he knew he wasn't old enough — not yet.

So he made a smiling snowman,

and he made angels.

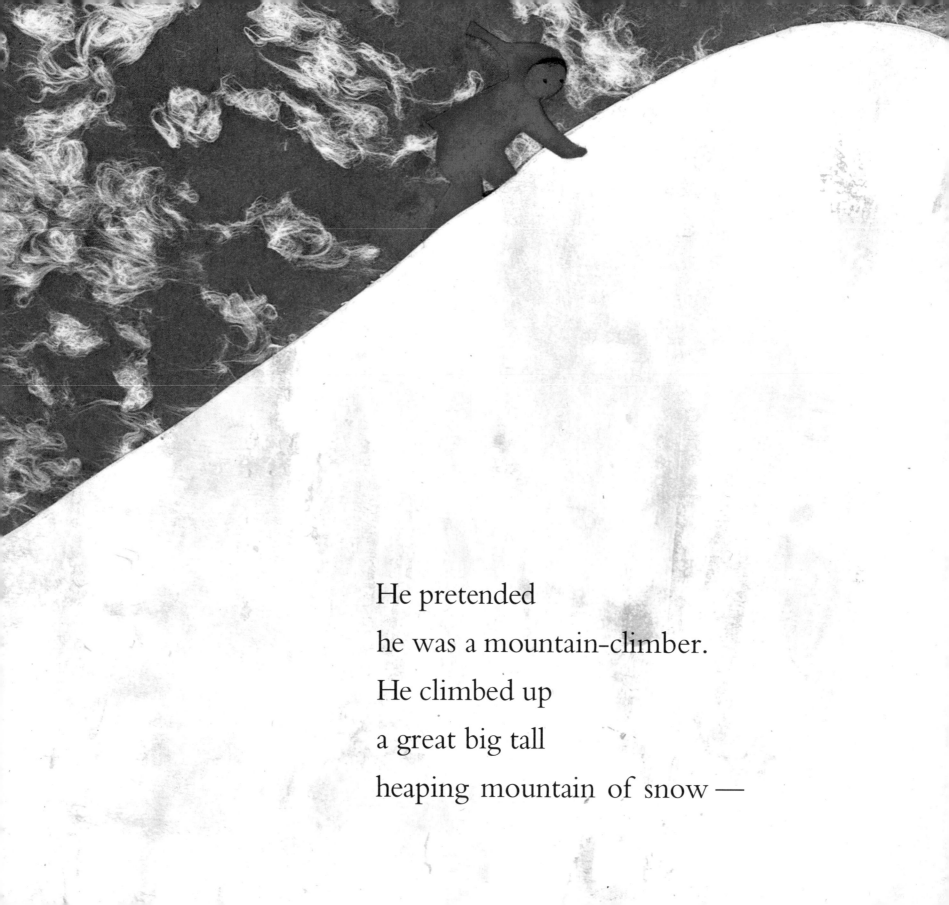

He pretended
he was a mountain-climber.
He climbed up
a great big tall
heaping mountain of snow —

and slid all the way down.

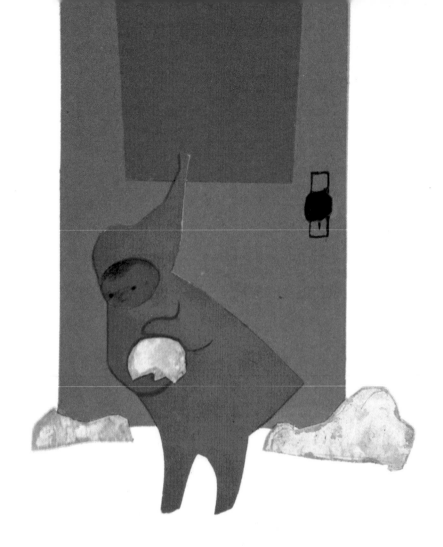

He picked up a handful of snow — and another, and still another. He packed it round and firm and put the snowball in his pocket for tomorrow. Then he went into his warm house.

He told his mother all about his adventures
while she took off his wet socks.

And he thought and thought
and thought about them.

Before he got into bed he looked in his pocket.

His pocket was empty. The snowball wasn't there.

He felt very sad.

While he slept, he dreamed that the sun
had melted all the snow away.

But when he woke up his dream was gone.

The snow was still everywhere.

New snow was falling!

After breakfast he called to his
friend from across the hall, and
they went out together into the
deep, deep snow.

Keats at work in his studio

The original clipping from a
1940 issue of *Life* magazine

O f all the characters that sprang from the mind of Ezra
Jack Keats, Peter, who first appeared in *The Snowy Day*,
remains the most widely beloved. Before this book came out
in the early 1960s, very few picture books had ever featured
African American characters. Years earlier, when Keats was beginning his career as an illustrator, he saw a set of photos of
a little black boy in *Life* magazine and stuck them up on the
wall of his studio. He hoped he'd be asked to illustrate a picture book about an African American child and could use the
photos for inspiration. But no opportunities to create such a
character came his way. The photos remained on his wall for
twenty-two years before Keats finally decided he would write
the book himself, and Peter and *The Snowy Day* were born.

Keats's initial sketch for the cover

The final cover image

The manuscript of *The Snowy Day*

Keats spent a long time working on the manuscript of *The Snowy Day* with his editor, Annis Duff. He had illustrated many books by then, but this was the first he had written entirely by himself. When it was finally finished, Keats had to decide how to illustrate the story. He knew that he wanted the artwork to be different from anything he'd created before. From the beginning, Keats thought he might like to incorporate a little patterned paper into the mostly painted illustrations. But the more he worked on the book, the more his collage style developed, and the more paper he found that made its way into the book. As he described it,

> *The creative efforts of people from many lands contributed to the materials in the book. Some of the papers used for the collage came from Japan, some from Italy, some from Sweden, many from our own country.*
>
> *The mother's dress is made of oil cloth used for lining cupboards. I made a big sheet of snow-texture. I used gum erasers to achieve the effect of snow flakes. I cut patterns of snow flakes, dipped them into paint and then stamped them onto the pages. The gray background for the pages where Peter goes to sleep was made by spattering India ink with a toothbrush.*

Keats said that when he showed the finished book to his artist friends, they couldn't believe he had created it, it was so different from his earlier work. But it set the tone for the style he would continue to use for the rest of his career.

Ezra Jack Keats
210 E. 58th Street
New York, N. Y.

March 27, 1964

Mrs. James Weldon Johnson
10 West 135th St.
New York 37, N. Y.

Dear Mrs. Johnson:

It may somewhat astonish you to receive
an acknowledgement of the letters you wrote
in the Spring of '63. In them you expressed
appreciation for my book, "the Snowy Day".
Of all the letters I received, yours were
among those that were especially meaningful
to me. Because at the time I received them
I was inundated by work and preoccupied with
personal matters so that I could not answer
kind notes such as yours.

May I take this occasion to thank you
for the support and profound encouragement
you have given me. My best wishes to you.

Sincerely,

Ezra Jack Keats

:dg

LANGSTON HUGHES
20 EAST 127TH STREET
NEW YORK 35, N. Y.

February 18, 1963

Dear Miss Crittenden:

THE SNOWY DAY by Ezra Jack Keats
is a perfectly charming little book.
I wish I had some grandchildren to give
it to. Yes, I do!

Sincerely yours,

Langston Hughes
Langston Hughes

Display for *The Snowy Day* in a bookstore window

Dear Mr Keats I like all of
your books.

Your friend,
Hollie

THE
SNOWY
DAY
BY
EZRA JACK KEATS

The Snowy Day was published in 1962. When it came out, readers and reviewers fell in love with the book. Many reviewers made comments like this one, from *The Baltimore Sun*: "The fact that the artist has pictured Peter as a Negro child, quite without making any particular point of it, is a pleasant surprise that adds a new dimension to picture book content."

Letters to Keats poured in from adults and children alike. He heard from the widow of the author and activist James Weldon Johnson, and from the poet Langston Hughes. And he received hundreds of letters from children and teachers about the book's impact on its youngest readers. According to *The Minneapolis Star*, "One elementary teacher wrote that before she read *The Snowy Day* to her class, also predominantly Negro, both white and Negro youngsters would use pink paint to represent themselves when painting pictures. After reading the story, the Negro children started using brown paint when painting pictures of themselves, Keats said. 'It gives them a sense of belonging. They are in books.'"

Said Keats, "I don't like to emphasize the race thing, because what's really important is the honesty."

In early 1963, Ezra Jack Keats received a long-distance phone call from Chicago, telling him he had won the Caldecott Award. He'd never heard of the award before, so he asked a few friends if they knew anything about it. They were surprised that Keats wasn't familiar with the biggest and most significant award for a children's book in the country.

Keats was euphoric about winning the Caldecott until he found out he'd have to deliver an acceptance speech in front of nearly two thousand teachers and librarians. He was terrified of speaking in public and worried he'd faint or start to cry. The evening of the banquet, Keats wandered around Chicago in a panicked daze. Luckily, a kindly young editor calmed Keats down and gently brought him to the banquet in his honor. Though he was too nervous to eat, once he stood at the dais he calmed down enough to deliver the speech he'd prepared. He talked about how his friends had helped him come up with the story:

> *Friends would enthusiastically discuss the things they did as children in the snow, others would suggest nuances of plot, or a change of a word here or there. All of us wanted so much to see little Peter march through these pages, experiencing, in the purity and innocence of childhood, the joy of a first snow.*

Keats was enormously proud of winning the award, but delivering the speech had been such an ordeal that it felt like an equally major accomplishment to him.

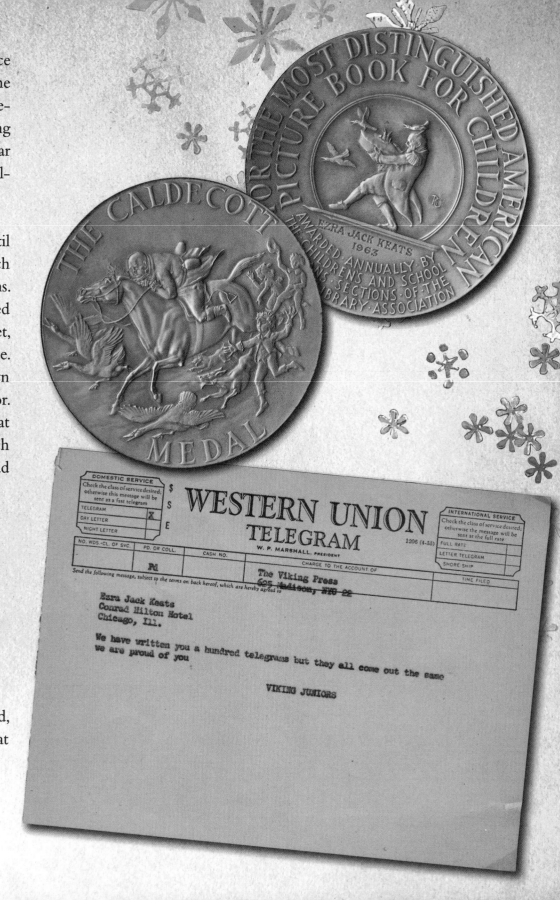

Keats (far left) at the Newbery Caldecott banquet with honored
guests including Madeleine L'Engle (second from right)

NEWBERY · CALDECOTT

AWARDS | DINNER

July 15, 1963

HONORING

AND

Madeleine L'Engle

Ezra Jack Keats

WINNER OF

WINNER OF

The Newbery Medal

The Caldecott Medal

FOR

FOR

A Wrinkle in Time

The Snowy Day

"The most distinguished contribution
to American literature for children"
published in 1962

"The most distinguished American
picture book for children"
published in 1962

A program from the Newbery Caldecott Awards dinner

The Snowy Day became one of the most beloved children's books of all time. It has been translated into at least ten languages and is popular all over the world. It has influenced award-winning authors and illustrators and inspired thousands of children to create artwork.

Ezra Jack Keats went on to create several more books about Peter, as well as other favorite characters such as Louie, Amy, and many more. The little strip of photos from *Life* magazine launched him into a world he never could have imagined in his early days as an illustrator. The experience of creating *The Snowy Day* changed Keats's life profoundly. As Keats said,

I realize now that we have so many levels of experience that even when we are despairing and we feel cut off and alone, other, life-saving forces are working through the sadness. Like strata of water in hard rock. Where do they come from? Sometimes I would feel that life was one vast desert, relentless, remorseless, and I could pick up a stone and water would spurt out. Hidden fountains of feeling we carry inside us, and we don't know it. I wonder what ripples of laughter and joy and love are buried—to surface one day just as the meaning of Peter's pictures had finally emerged for me. '

Keats signing books for children in Japan

The Snowy Day in:

Japanese

French

Spanish

Chinese

Korean